To my dear father,
who never got to see Olivia
in the flesh or in print

SIMON AND SCHUSTER

First published in Great Britain in 2007 by Simon & Schuster UK Ltd

1st Floor, 222 Gray's Inn Road, London, WC1X 8HB

A CBS company

This paperback edition published in 2014

Originally published in 2007 by Atheneum Books for Young Readers,

an imprint of Simon & Schuster Children's Publishing Division, New York

Book design by Ann Bobco

The text for this book is set in Centaur

The illustrations for this book are rendered in charcoal and goache on paper

A CIP catalogue record for this book is available from the British Library

978-1-4711-2310-8

Printed in China

1 2 3 4 5 6 7 8 9 10

www.simonandschuster.co.uk

OLIVIA
helps with Christmas

by Ian Falconer

SIMON AND SCHUSTER
LONDON   NEW YORK   SYDNEY   TORONTO   NEW DELHI

'Twas the day before Christmas. Olivia and her family had been out all morning, busy with last-minute shopping.

Olivia was exhausted,
yet there was still so
much to do.

Olivia told her father and Ian to put up the tree,

so she could help her mother with William's lunch.

"Olivia, what are you feeding him?"

"Blueberry pie."

"Oh, darling,
that's going to
make him . . .

. . . sick!"

"Whoops."

By four o'clock Olivia was getting impatient.

"Sweetheart, Santa won't be here for hours,"
said her mother. "Now, wipe that soot off
your snout and help me untangle these lights."

"MUMMY!"

"Darling, it's much easier if you plug
them in first. There, isn't that better?"

Finally the tree was trimmed.

. . . . . 5:00 PM . . . . SANTA WATCH . . . . NO SANTA . . . . RAIN . . .

"Why, that's beautiful, darling. Where
did you ever find that perfect little . . .

. . . tree?"

Olivia wanted to be even more of a help. "Mummy, may I set the table for Christmas Eve dinner?"

"Oh yes, Olivia, that would be very helpful."

Olivia's father came in to build a fire.

"DADDY! WHAT COULD YOU BE THINKING? DO YOU WANT TO COOK SANTA?!"

. . 7:00 PM . . . . SANTA WATCH . . . . NO SANTA . . . . (BUT NO RAIN) . . .

After dinner the family gathered to sing carols.
Softly they started: "Angels we have heard on high,
sweetly singing o'er the plains."

Olivia always lets go for the chorus.

Glo-oooo-O-ri-a!

Finally the most important task of the
night: leaving treats for Santa Claus.

Olivia said, "Now it's time to wait." Her mother said, "Now it's time for bed."

But Olivia wasn't at all sleepy.

She tossed . . .

and she turned.

First she was hot.

Then she was cold.

Then she heard something on the roof.

Could it be Santa???

It seemed she would never get to sleep—
until she woke up and saw it was morning.
Olivia ran to get her brothers.

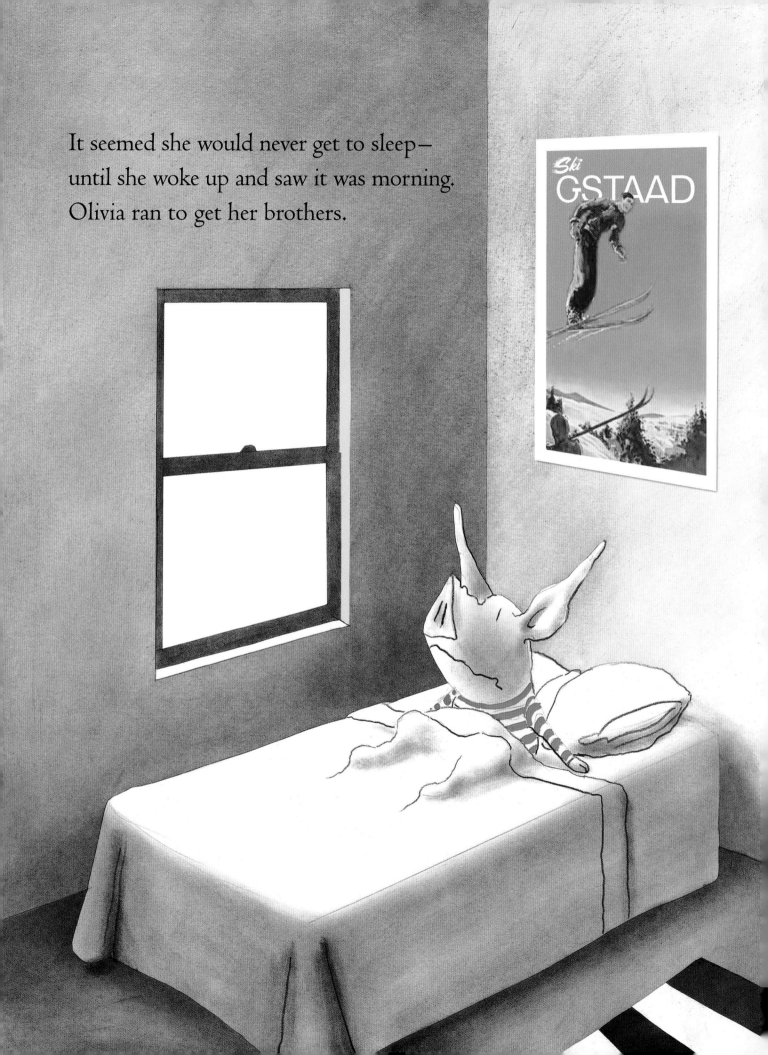

Noiselessly they crept down the stairs.

SNOW!

PRESENTS!

STOCKINGS!

"And look!" cried Olivia.
"Santa ate all the cookies
and milk!"

For
SANTA

BURP!

"Now, children," said Olivia's mother. "Finish your breakfast, and then you can open your presents under the . . .

"It looks like someone just learned to walk."

Some of Santa's offerings were better than others.

Pyjamas.

Skis!

Sweater.

Sledge!

Booties.

Maracas!

. . . tree."

The children thanked their parents for a
wonderful Christmas and Olivia announced,
"Now I have a present for *you.*"

"It's a self-portrait. Won't it be beautiful over the fireplace?"

"Well," said Olivia, "I think I'll hit the slopes."

"Skiing takes more practice."

Olivia and Ian worked all afternoon to make a snowman.

Olivia dressed it.

That evening Olivia finally allowed her father to build a fire. The family sat and warmed their trotters while Olivia's mother brought them steaming mugs of hot soup.

Soon it was time for bed, but Olivia wasn't at all sleepy.

Or so she said. But before the lights were even out, she fell into a deep, dreamless slumber . . .

Well, not quite dreamless.